P9-DEZ-074

Bobby Bear

BY CHARLES GHIGNA
ILLUSTRATED BY JACQUELINE EAST

PICTURE WINDOW BOOKS
a capstone imprint

For Charlotte Rose

Tiny Tales are published by Picture Window Books,
a Capstone imprint
1710 Roe Crest Drive
North Mankato, Minnesota 56003
www.capstonepub.com

Library of Congress Cataloging-in-Publication Data
Ghigna, Charles, author. Bobby Bear / by Charles Ghigna ;
illustrated by Jacqueline East.
pages cm. -- (Tiny tales)
Summary: In five simple stories, Bobby Bear enjoys a day at the
lake, a slumber party, and other activities with his family and
friends.
ISBN 978-1-4795-6531-3 (library binding)
ISBN 978-1-4795-6535-1 (paperback)
ISBN 978-1-4795-8482-6 (eBook)

1. Bears--Juvenile fiction. 2. Animals--Juvenile fiction. 3. Families-
-Juvenile fiction. [1. Bears--Fiction. 2. Animals--Fiction. 3. Family
life--Fiction.] I. East, Jacqueline, illustrator. II. Title.

PZ7.G3390234Bo 2016
[E]--dc23   2014045630

Designer: Kristi Carlson

Printed in the United States of America in Stevens Point, Wisconsin.
032015   008824WZF15

table of contents

1

A Picnic at the Lake

One sunny day, Bobby Bear and his mother decided to have a picnic by the lake. They spread out a red blanket, opened their picnic basket, and sat down to eat.

After lunch, they napped in the shade of a big oak tree. When Bobby Bear woke up, he strolled down to the lake.

Bobby Bear looked into the surface of the water and jumped back. He could not believe his eyes! There, in the water, was another little bear staring up at him.

"Oh, my," he said to himself. "There is another little bear! And he is in the lake."

Bobby Bear sat down on the shore and thought.

"I know," he said. "I will jump in the lake and join him!"

Bobby Bear took a deep breath and jumped in. He saw a turtle, an old shoe, and a school of minnows. But no matter where he looked, Bobby Bear could not find the other little bear.

"Oh, my," he said to himself. "I must have scared him away."

Bobby Bear swam back to the shore and sat down. He waited for the other little bear to come out of the lake.

He sat and he waited. And waited. And waited.

Bobby Bear wondered where the other little bear had gone. He decided to take another look in the lake.

He leaned over and looked in. There he was again!

Bobby Bear took a deep breath and jumped in. Again, he could not find the other little bear.

"Oh, my," he said to himself.
"That little bear can swim fast.
I wonder where he went?"

Bobby Bear swam back to the
shore. His mother was waiting
for him.

On the way home, Bobby Bear told his mother about the little bear he saw in the lake. His mother smiled and listened.

"What was the little bear wearing?" she asked.

"Pants and a shirt, just like mine," said Bobby Bear.

"And what color were the little bear's shirt?" she asked.

"It was green, just like mine," he said.

"And what color was the little bear's pants?" she asked.

"They were blue, just like mine," Bobby Bear said.

"It sounds like you found your twin," his mother said, smiling.

Bobby Bear thought for a moment. Then he smiled and said,

"Oh, my! That was ME I saw in the lake. It was like I was looking into a mirror!"

Bobby Bear and his mother laughed and laughed all the way home.

② Slumber Party

Tonight was Bobby Bear's first slumber party. All of his friends were on their way to his house. He had been so excited the night before that he could hardly sleep.

Bobby Bear was in the kitchen when the doorbell rang. He raced to the door. He was happy to see all of his friends.

Oliver Owl, Benny Bunny, Scotty Squirrel, and Peter Possum dropped their bags and pillows at the door. Then they started a game of tag around the couch.

Bobby Bear's mother quickly sent them outside for a game of hide-and-seek.

Benny Bunny hopped behind a bush. Scotty Squirrel scampered up a tree. Peter Possum pretended he was asleep in the garden. Oliver Owl hid in a big tree.

Bobby Bear stood with his eyes closed, counting to twenty. He was at number nineteen when he heard the doorbell ring. It was the pizza!

Everyone hurried out of their hiding
places. They headed for the picnic table.

Bobby Bear's mother brought out
a tray with juice, chips, and grapes.
Bobby Bear's father brought out two
large pizzas. The night smelled of
pepperoni and cheese.

After dinner and more games, everyone went inside. They got into pajamas, brushed their teeth, and spread out their sleeping bags.

When they were all tucked in, Bobby Bear's mother said, "Before you all fall asleep, would you like to play Sweet Dreams?"

"What's that?" asked Oliver Owl.

"It's a game where you take turns saying something you like best. It helps everyone fall asleep and have sweet dreams," she said, smiling. "For example, I like being a mom the best."

Benny Bunny said, "I like Easter best!"

Peter Possum said, "I like Christmas best!"

Oliver Owl said, "I like Halloween best!"

Scotty Squirrel said, "I like slumber parties best!"

Now it was Bobby Bear's turn. Everyone was quietly waiting to hear what he liked best.

After a long silence, his mother finally asked, "Bobby Bear, what do you like best?"

But Bobby Bear did not answer. He was already fast asleep.

Everyone quietly giggled as they closed their eyes and drifted off to sweet dreams.

3

Animals in the Sky

Bobby Bear loved going to the park with his father. There was always so much to do.

It was fun swinging on the swings and sliding down the slide. He liked the big playhouse in the center of the park. It had a fireman's pole in the middle. He liked climbing up the ladder and sliding down the pole.

Today he liked finding shapes in
the clouds with his father.

"That one looks like a lion!"
Bobby said.

"It sure does," said his father.
"It even has a tail!"

Bobby pointed at another cloud.
"I think that cloud looks like a giraffe,"
he said.

"Yes, it does," said his father. "And
it has a very long neck!"

"There's one
that looks like
an elephant!"
said Bobby.

"You are
an excellent shape
finder!" said his father.

"I love the park," said Bobby.

"I love the park, too," said his father as they sat down on a park bench. Just then, a big white cloud drifted overhead.

"What shape is that cloud?" asked his father.

"That one looks like a polar bear!" said Bobby.

"And look at that one," said his father.

Bobby said, "That one looks like a hippopotamus."

Bobby Bear pointed to another cloud. "And that one looks like a crocodile."

"And that one looks like a walrus," said his father.

"That's the funniest looking walrus I've ever seen," said Bobby Bear.

It was getting late. Bobby Bear and his father started heading back home.

"Where would you like to go tomorrow?" his father asked.

"I don't know," Bobby said.

"How about we go some place and see all the clouds come to life?" his father asked.

"Where in the world is that?" Bobby asked.

"I'll give you a hint," said his father. "Where do people go to see many different kinds of animals, like the ones we've seen today in the clouds?"

"Oh, I know where we are going tomorrow," said Bobby Bear. "We are going to the zoo!"

"We sure are," his father said, smiling.

The Bike Parade

Bobby Bear loved riding his tricycle. He spent all afternoon riding. He would go back and forth under the big trees in front of his house.

The tree shadows made a pattern on the sidewalk that looked like railroad tracks. Bobby pretended his trike was a train.

"Choo-choo! Choo-choo!" he said.

Just then, Bobby saw his friend Billy Bear coming down the sidewalk. Billy was older than Bobby. He was riding his new two-wheel bicycle.

"I wish I could ride a big bike," Bobby said.

Bobby Bear imagined himself riding a big bike. He was lost in his thoughts when Billy Bear rode up next to him.

"How's it going?" asked Billy Bear.

"Great!" said Bobby Bear. "I like your new bike."

"Thanks," said Billy Bear. "And I like your tricycle."

"Really?" said Bobby Bear. "I wish I could ride a big bike like you."

"I just learned," Billy said. "You will learn soon, too."

"I sure hope so," said Bobby. "Your bike is just so cool."

"Your tricycle is pretty cool, too," Billy said.

"It is?" Bobby asked.

"It sure is! The streamers are awesome, and I really like the flag," Billy said.

"You do?" said Bobby Bear.

"Yes, I do," said Billy Bear. "I really like your horn!"

Bobby Bear tooted his horn for Billy. They both laughed.

"When I rode a tricycle, my friends
and I would have bicycle parades,"
said Billy Bear. "We would ride up
and down the sidewalk all day."

"That's a great idea!" Bobby said.

Just then, Hannah Bear and Emily Bear rode up on their tricycles.

"Hi," said Bobby Bear. "Would you like to join my parade?"

"What parade?" asked Hannah Bear, looking around.

"The one we are going to make," said Bobby Bear. "Follow me!"

Hannah Bear and Emily Bear joined in, pedaling behind Bobby Bear on their tricycles. The afternoon shadows from the trees had grown long across the sidewalk.

"It looks like we're riding on a railroad track," said Emily Bear.

"Choo-choo! Choo-choo!" said Bobby Bear.

"Choo-choo! Choo-choo!" said Hannah and Emily.

Hannah and Emily proudly followed Bobby Bear down the sidewalk in their tricycle parade.

Bobby Bear was no longer sad he couldn't ride a big bike. In fact, Bobby Bear had never been happier!

5

Camping in the Woods

Bobby Bear and his dad loved spending time outside. And they really loved camping in the woods.

It was fun cooking over the fire and listening to the crickets. They enjoyed watching the fireflies and looking up at the stars.

"There are so many amazing things to see in the night sky," said his dad.

Bobby Bear and his dad sat quietly, looking up at the sky. It was a clear night. The sky was full of stars.

"See those stars that look like a cup with a long handle?" asked his dad.

"Yes, I see them!" said Bobby.

"That's called the Big Dipper," said his dad. "And those stars over there are the Little Dipper."

"Cool!" said Bobby.

"All this stargazing is making me hungry," said his dad.

"Me too!" said Bobby.

Bobby Bear's dad cooked hot dogs
over the fire. Bobby snacked on grapes
while he waited.

"The hot dogs are finally done,"
his dad said.

He put the warm hot dog in a bun and squeezed some ketchup on it.

"Here you go!" he said.

"Mmmmm," said Bobby. "Delicious!"

"I agree," his dad said.

When they finished eating their hot dogs, Bobby Bear and his dad toasted marshmallows on a stick.

His dad put a toasted marshmallow on a graham cracker and added a piece of chocolate.

"Try this," his dad said.

"Wow!" said Bobby. "That is so
yummy! Can I have some more?"

"That's what they're called," said
his dad.

"What?" asked Bobby.

"S'mores. That's what the treat is called. It's called a s'more because every time you eat one, you always want some more!" his dad said

"I get it," Bobby said, smiling.

After a few more treats and some stories, Bobby Bear yawned.

"Looks like someone's getting sleepy," said his dad. "Let's get in the tent."

"Sounds good," said Bobby.

Bobby Bear took one long last look up at the stars and started singing, "Twinkle, twinkle, little star. How I wonder what you are. Up above the world so high, like a diamond in the sky. Twinkle, twinkle, little star. How I wonder what you are."

"The perfect goodnight song," said his dad.

"I love camping with you," said Bobby Bear.

"Me too," said his dad. "Me too."

GLOSSARY

camping (KAMP-ing) — living and sleeping outdoors for a little while, usually in tents or in cabins

drifted (DRIFT-ed) — gently carried or moved by the wind or water

minnows (MIN-ohz) — very small fish that live in lakes, ponds, and other freshwater

parade (puh-RADE) — a line of people, vehicles, and other things that go through the streets, usually to celebrate something

pattern (PAT-urn) — repeating shapes and colors

picnic (PIK-nik) — a party or trip that includes eating a meal or snacks outdoors scampered (SKAM-purd) — ran quickly and lightly

shore (SHOR) — the land along the edge of a river, pond, lake, sea, or ocean

slumber party (SLUHM-bur PAHR-tee) — a party where children all go to one person's house and sleep there for the night

stargazing (STARH-gayz-ing) — looking up at the stars at night

strolled (STROHLD) — walked in a slow and relaxed way

surface (SUR-fiss) — the very top or outside part of something

toasted (TOHST-ed) — warmed up enough that the outside of the food gets brown

DISCUSSION QUESTIONS

1. Bobby Bear and his dad like to go camping. They like looking up at the stars, cooking hot dogs, and making s'mores. What things would you do on a camping trip?

2. Have you ever tried to find shapes in the clouds like Bobby and his dad? What kinds of shapes did you see?

3. Bobby was so excited for the slumber party, but he fell asleep early! Why do you think he fell asleep? What could he have done to stay awake?

4. Billy Bear's two-wheel bicycle was really cool, but Bobby needs to practice more before he can ride a big bike. Talk about something that you want to learn how to do one day.

5. Bobby spent a lot of time looking at the sky. What do you like more, looking for shapes in clouds or looking at the stars? Why?

6. Bobby has fun doing things with his parents, like camping with Dad or going to the lake with Mom. What are some of your favorite things to do with your parents or family?

Writing Prompts

1. There are lots of things you can do at the park. Bobby likes to go down the fireman's pole and look at the clouds. Write a list of things that you do when you visit a park or playground.

2. Bobby Bear and his dad are going to go to the zoo. Write a story about their trip. What kind of animals did they see?

3. Bobby and his friends had fun making their own bike parade. Write about a fun game you like to play with your friends.

4. Imagine you're having your own slumber party, and make an invitation for your party. Be sure to write what games you'll play and what food you'll eat!

5. Bobby and his mom had a good time at their picnic by the lake. What kind of things would you take to a picnic? Write about what food you would have, who would come with you, and where you would go.

6. Play Sweet Dreams and think of what you like best. Draw a picture of it and write a few sentences explaining why you like it best.

Author Bio

Charles Ghigna (also known as Father Goose®) lives in a tree house in Alabama. He is the author of more than 100 award-winning books for children and adults from Random House, Capstone, Disney, Hyperion, Scholastic, Simon & Schuster, Abrams, Charlesbridge, and other publishers.

His poems appear in hundreds of magazines, from *The New Yorker* and *Harper's* to *Cricket* and *Highlights*. He is a former poetry editor of the *English Journal* and nationally syndicated feature writer for Tribune Media Services.

Illustrator Bio

Jacqueline East has been illustrating children's books for many years. Her work has been published across the globe and is known for its warm innocence and humor. Everything is an inspiration, and she especially loves the golden atmosphere of twilight; a magical time of day that is often the backdrop for her characters.

She has worked above a chocolate factory, in a caravan by the sea, and now, from her home in Bristol with Scampi the dog sleeping in the corner of the studio!